P9-DGL-435

Here's what kids have to say to
Mary Pope Osborne, author of
the Magic Tree House series:

*Your books are so, so, so magical that I refuse
to get any other books from the library.*
—Ben H.

*I love the Magic Tree House books. My Daddy
and I have read all of them.*—Kevin F.

Me and my Mom really love your books.
—Julie P.

*Every time I finish your books I want to read
them over and over again because it is so
much fun.*—Soo Jin K.

*I'm going to write just like you when I grow
up.*—Raul A.

*Out of all the books in the world, yours are the
best. I hope your books will never end.*
—Karina D.

*You could really read my mind—wherever
Jack and Annie go, I want to go.*
—Matthew D.

Parents and teachers love
Magic Tree House books, too!

I wish to thank you for creating this series, as you have given every teacher who passionately loves to read a vehicle for enticing young children to discover the magic of books.—K. Salkaln

My students <u>love</u> your Magic Tree House books. In fact, there is a reading craze in our classroom, thanks to your wonderful books!—S. Tcherepnin

I would like to say that your books are wonderful. I have never found any other educational books that were so interesting to my students.—C. Brewer

Kevin got two of your books with a gift certificate. He read the whole way home and did not come up for air until he had completed both books.—K. Trostle

I have been trying for years to find a book that students would enjoy and be crazy about. Most books do not capture the attention of students like your books do. Even my boys say, "Please do not stop reading." It is a pleasure to find something the students will read that is worthwhile and wholesome. I applaud you.
—L. Kirl

You have opened the door to adventures for some, and others want to follow in your footsteps as authors. Thank you for creating and sharing that magical world of the imagination.—M. Hjort

My son has always struggled when reading. Since discovering your books, he has a new desire to read.—M. Casameny

Dear Readers,

Your letters continue to help me write the Magic Tree House series.

   One day while I was writing <u>Lions at Lunchtime</u>, I got stuck—I couldn't figure out what should happen when Jack and Annie get caught by the Masai warrior. Finally, I decided to take a break and read some letters from you. I read a letter from a boy named Mark, who lives in Massachusetts. He had written to suggest that Jack and Annie decide to visit the tree house on their way home from the grocery store. A light bulb went on in my head, and I figured out a way Jack and Annie could make friends with the warrior.

   Thank you, Mark. Thanks to all you readers. Your enthusiasm for the series keeps me writing more books.

   All my best,

Mary Pope Osborne

Lions at Lunchtime

by Mary Pope Osborne
illustrated by Sal Murdocca

SCHOLASTIC INC.
New York Toronto London Auckland Sydney

To Shana Corey,
with appreciation for all her help

No part of this publication may be reproduced in whole or in part, or stored in a retrieval system, or transmitted in any form or by any means, electronic, mechanical, photocopying, recording, or otherwise, without written permission of the publisher. For information regarding permission, write to Random House, 201 East 50th Street, New York, NY 10022.

ISBN 0-590-70637-3

Copyright © 1998 by Mary Pope Osborne. Illustrations copyright © 1998 by Sal Murdocca. All rights reserved. Published by Scholastic Inc., 555 Broadway, New York, NY 10012, by arrangement with Random House, Inc. SCHOLASTIC and associated logos are trademarks and/or registered trademarks of Scholastic Inc.

12 11 10 9 8 7 6 5 4 3 2   8 9/9 0 1 2 3/0

Printed in the U.S.A.   40

First Scholastic printing, November 1998

Contents

1
Before Lunch

Jack and Annie were walking home from the grocery store. Jack's pack was heavy. It held a big jar of peanut butter and a loaf of bread.

"Are you going to have a peanut butter and jelly sandwich?" said Annie. "Or a peanut butter and honey sandwich?"

Jack started to answer, but stopped.

"Oh, man," he whispered.

"What is it?" said Annie.

"Look at *that!*" said Jack.

He pointed to the edge of the Frog Creek woods. In the shadows stood a small, delicate animal. It looked like a tiny deer.

"It's a sign," whispered Annie. "Remember when we saw the rabbit? He was a sign of the Wild West."

The deerlike creature leaped into the woods.

Jack and Annie didn't stop to think. They followed as fast as they could. Jack's heavy pack thumped against his back as he ran.

Finally, they stopped and looked around.

"Where did she go?" he said.

"I don't see her," said Annie.

"Oh, wow," said Annie. She pointed up.

There was the magic tree house. It was shining in the noon sun, at the top of the tallest tree in the woods. Its rope ladder swayed in the shadows below.

"Where's Morgan?" said Annie.

Morgan le Fay wasn't waving at them from the window. She wasn't even at the window.

"I don't know. Let's go up," said Jack.

They climbed the ladder and went into the tree house.

Sunlight streamed through the window. It lit a stack of books and two scrolls in the corner. The ancient scrolls held the answers to riddles Jack and Annie had solved earlier.

Jack took off his heavy pack.

"Did Morgan leave us a third riddle?" said Annie.

"Looking for someone?" said a soft voice.

Jack and Annie whirled around.

"Morgan!" said Annie.

Morgan le Fay had appeared out of nowhere. She looked ancient and lovely in the bright light.

"Do you still want to become Master Librarians?" she asked Jack and Annie. "So you can help me in my work?"

"Yes!" they said together.

"Wonderful," Morgan said. Then she reached into her robe and pulled out a scroll.

"You've solved two riddles so far," she said. "Here is your third." She handed the

scroll to Annie. "And for your research—"

She pulled a book out from her robe and handed it to Jack. The book's cover said THE PLAINS OF AFRICA.

"*Africa?*" said Jack. "Oh, man, I've always wanted to go there."

He opened the book. He and Annie stared at a picture.

It showed hordes of zebras, tall giraffes, big animals with horns, and tiny, deerlike creatures.

"Hey, that's the animal that led us here!" said Annie.

"A Thomson's gazelle, I believe," Morgan said.

"Where are the lions?" said Jack.

"You'll find out," said Morgan.

"Um...maybe we need to plan this trip," said Jack.

Morgan smiled. "No. Go ahead. Make your wish now."

Annie pointed at the picture. "I wish we

could go there," she said.

"Be careful," said Morgan. "Just keep an eye out."

"For what?" said Jack.

"The lions, of course," she said.

"Wait!" said Jack.

Too late.

The wind had started to blow.

The tree house had started to spin.

Jack squeezed his eyes shut.

The tree house spun faster and faster.

Then everything was still.

Absolutely still.

2

Jump, Beasts! Jump!

Bright light flooded the tree house again. A rustling sound came from outside the window.

Annie peeked out and laughed. "Hey, there," she said.

Jack looked out, too. A giraffe was eating leaves off the tree. It had a sweet, goofy face.

Jack peered at the world beyond the giraffe. He couldn't believe his eyes.

He saw a huge grassy plain, a wide river, and *tons* of birds and animals—more than he had ever imagined in one place.

Giraffes and zebras were on the side of the river where Jack and Annie were. Thomson's gazelles and the big horned animals were on the other side.

"Where are the lions?" said Jack.

"I don't know," said Annie. "Do you think it's always this crowded?"

"Let's find out," said Jack.

He picked up the book on Africa and looked at the picture of the animals. He read aloud:

> Every year, in late spring, thousands
> of zebras and gazelles and millions
> of wildebeests (WILL-duh-beests)
> migrate from the dry plains of
> Tanzania to Kenya.

"What's 'migrate' mean?" said Annie.

Jack pushed his glasses into place. "It means they go someplace else for part of the year—like birds going south for the winter."

"Oh, right," said Annie.

Jack turned the page to read more.

> Before they are safe in Kenya, the animals must first cross the Mara River. Zebras go first, then the wildebeests. The tiny gazelles swim last.

"Ohh," said Annie in a sad voice.

"What's wrong?" said Jack.

"Poor beasts." She looked out the window. "They seem afraid."

On the far side of the river, the horned animals were standing at the edge of the steep bank of the river. They stared down nervously at the rushing water.

"Jump, beasts! Jump!" Annie shouted.

"Don't be silly. They can't hear you," said Jack.

He studied the broad plain. "I wonder where the lions are," he said.

"I don't know. But I have to go," said Annie.

"Go *where?*" said Jack.

"To the river to help them," she said.

"Help *who?*" said Jack.

"Those wild beasts on the other side!" said Annie. "I have to help them *migrate.*"

"Are you nuts?" said Jack.

Annie handed Jack the scroll and started out of the tree house.

"Wait a second!" said Jack. "We haven't even read Morgan's riddle yet!"

Annie stopped on the ladder.

"Read it now," she said.

Jack unrolled the ancient scroll and read aloud:

> I'm the color of gold
> and as sweet as can be.
> But beware of the danger
> that's all around me.
> What am I?

Annie started down again.

"Annie!"

"We'll look for the answer in a minute," said Annie.

"What are you doing?" Jack called.

But there was no stopping her. Jack watched as she hopped off the ladder. Then she started to walk through the tall grass, between the zebras and giraffes.

"I don't believe her," he said to himself. He quickly put the Africa book into his pack.

He started down the ladder.

When he stepped onto the ground, he looked around carefully.

The giraffes were eating the tree leaves.

The zebras were grazing in the grass.

Tons of birds flapped overhead.

This is okay, he thought. He just had one little question:

Where are the lions?

3

Disaster

"Come on, Jack!" Annie called. She was almost to the river.

"Just a minute!" he shouted. He wanted to study the giraffes and zebras.

He pulled out the Africa book and found a picture of giraffes. He read:

> The giraffe is the tallest animal in the world. Its legs alone can be six feet tall, and its hooves can be as big as dinner plates. The giraffe has

a very powerful kick, which makes it
dangerous to attack. For this reason,
lions tend to avoid giraffes.

Jack pulled out his notebook and wrote:

Notes on Africa
_____

lions avoid ginaffes

He turned the page and read more:

Zebras live in family groups. As no two
zebras have exactly the same pattern
of stripes, every baby zebra must learn
its own mother's pattern.

Jack studied the zebras, trying to see their
different patterns. But in the hazy afternoon
light, all the stripes made him dizzy.

He blinked to clear his head, then read
more:

Zebras are the first to cross the river because they eat the coarsest grass. After they've thinned down the top layer, the wildebeests arrive and eat the next layer. They prepare the grass for the gazelles, who come last.

Wow, thought Jack. *Each animal depends on the one that goes before.*

He wrote:

animals all connected

Jack heard Annie shouting from the river-bank. "Jump, beasts! Jump! You can do it! Don't be afraid! Come on!"

He looked up. Annie herself was jumping as she called to the wildebeests.

Jack sighed. *I'd better stop her before there's trouble*, he thought.

He put away the Africa book and his note-book. Then he jogged toward the river. His pack was heavy and lumpy, bumping against his back. He'd forgotten to take out the jar of peanut butter and the loaf of bread.

Jack decided to leave them at the tree house. He turned to go back.

But just then, Annie's shouting stopped.

Jack looked at the river.

She had vanished.

"Annie?" he called.

No answer.

Where was she?

"Annie!" Jack shouted.

She had completely disappeared.

"Oh, man," said Jack.

Their trip had barely begun, and already disaster had struck!

He forgot about the stuff in his pack. He just ran as fast as he could.

He wove his way between the grazing zebras and giraffes as he raced to the river.

"Help!" called Annie.

4

Mud Bath

Jack looked over the edge of the riverbank.

Annie had fallen into a pool of mud near the water. The thick black mud was up to her chest.

"I slipped," she said. "It feels like quicksand."

Jack threw down his pack and got on his knees.

"Be careful," said Annie. "Don't slip, too."

Jack pointed to a tangle of old tree roots

sticking out of the bank. "Grab those!" he said.

Annie reached for the roots. "Too far," she said, breathing hard. "I'm sinking."

She *was* sinking. The mud was up to her neck.

"Hold on!" Jack looked around wildly. He saw a fallen tree branch near the bank.

He raced to it, picked it up, and carried it back to Annie. Only her head and arms stuck out of the mud now.

Jack held out the branch. Annie grabbed it.

"Hold tight," said Jack. "I'll drag you over to the roots!"

He started pulling on the branch.

"I'm still sinking!" Annie wailed. The mud was up to her chin.

"Come on!" said Jack. "You can do it! I know you can! Try! Try!"

Just then, Jack heard a *splash!* He looked up.

On the other side of the wide river, a wildebeest had jumped into the water. Another jumped...then another. They were headed right toward Jack and Annie.

"Hold on tight!" said Jack. He pulled on the stick again.

Annie moved a tiny bit.

"Hey, Jack, on the moon it felt like I weighed ten pounds," said Annie. "And in this mud it feels like I weigh a ton."

"Concentrate, Annie," said Jack, trying not to slip down the bank.

"I *am*."

The lead wildebeests were halfway across,

swimming toward them. Many more wilde-beests were jumping into the water.

"It's now or never!" said Jack. He took a deep breath. He pulled *really* hard.

Just then, a shadow passed over them. Jack looked up.

"Uh-oh," he said.

A huge vulture circled overhead.

"It thinks you're near the end," said Jack.

"Oh, get out of here!" Annie shouted at the vulture. "I'm fine!"

In a burst of fury, she let go of the branch. She lunged for the roots. She grabbed them!

"Yes!" cried Jack. "Pull! Pull!"

Slowly, Annie pulled herself out. She was covered with the black mud from head to toe.

Jack helped her onto the bank, getting mud all over himself.

"See!" Annie shook her fist at the vulture. "I'm fine! Now beat it!"

But the giant, ugly bird still circled.

"Come on. Let's get away from him," said Jack. He pushed his glasses into place.

"Rats," he said. Now his glasses were muddy.

He tried to clean his hands in the grass.

"Oh, no!" shouted Annie.

Jack turned to her.

"The wildebeests will get stuck in the mudhole!" she cried. She waved her arms at the wildebeests struggling to swim across the river.

"Not here," she shouted. "Not here!"

But the frantic swimmers kept coming.

5

Ha-Ha

"Oh, no! No! No!" shouted Annie.

She raced down the bank, until she reached a sandy, clear spot.

"Here! Here!" she called.

The wildebeests followed her with their wild eyes.

Jack watched in disbelief as the swimmers changed their course. Slowly, all the wildebeests swam to where Annie stood. She waved them in like a traffic policeman.

Jack grabbed his backpack.

"Annie," he cried, "let's go before we get trampled!"

"Keep it up," she shouted to the wildebeests as she took off after Jack.

They ran farther up the river, away from the incoming wildebeests. Finally, they stopped to catch their breath. They looked back.

Everything seemed fine. The wildebeests were scrambling safely over the riverbank. Soon they would graze on the grass prepared by the zebras.

"Good work," Jack said to Annie.

"Thanks," she said. "Okay, now for our riddle..."

"No, *first* we've got to get clean," said Jack. "You look like you're in a mud suit."

High-pitched laughter rang through the air. It sounded mocking and mean.

Jack and Annie turned around. They saw two spotted brown animals standing in the tall grass.

The creatures had bodies like dogs, but with sloping backs. They laughed again.

"Ha-ha," said Annie. "You don't look so great yourself."

"What are they?" said Jack. He took out the book. He tried not to get mud on it as he looked for a picture. When he found it, he read aloud:

> On the African plains, the hyena
> (hi-EE-nuh) is the ruling predator after
> the lion. It makes a sound similar to a
> high-pitched human laugh.

"What's 'predator' mean?" said Annie.

"It means it catches things and eats them," said Jack.

"Oh," said Annie. "Yuck."

The two hyenas laughed again. And they moved closer to Jack and Annie.

Quietly, Jack read more:

> **The hyena has a reputation for being a thief and a coward.**

"Let's see if they're cowards," whispered Annie. "Let's try to scare them."

The hyenas laughed and moved a little closer.

"How?" Jack asked.

"Act like a monster!" said Annie. "Now!"

Jack and Annie made terrible monster faces. They put out their hands and rushed at the hyenas.

"*ARGGGGHH!*" they shouted.

The hyenas yelped and scurried off.

"Scaredy-cats!" Annie shouted after them.

"Come on," said Jack.

Annie and Jack took off in the other direction. They ran around a bend in the river.

Jack heard the hyena laughter again. It sounded far away.

"Good," he said, "they're gone."

"Hey, maybe we can wash over there," said Annie.

She pointed to the edge of the forest. There was a small pond surrounded by tall grass. Zebras were drinking the water.

"Yeah," said Jack. "If it's safe enough for them to drink..."

The zebras ignored them as they walked toward the pond.

When they reached the edge of the water, Jack set his heavy pack down in the dry grass. He glanced around. No lions were in sight. But then he heard something.

On the far side of the pond, something very big was coming out of the trees.

6

Spick-and-Span

"Be still," said Jack.

Jack and Annie stood frozen as an elephant stepped out of the shadows. It waded into the pond and dipped its trunk into the water.

"Oh, wow," said Annie.

Jack breathed a sigh of relief. An elephant wasn't going to chase them and eat them. Still, the elephant was *huge*.

"Let's sneak away," said Jack.

"But I want to watch," said Annie.

"Fine," said Jack. He was tired of Annie getting sidetracked. "I'm going to solve the

riddle by myself. I'll meet you back at the tree house."

He turned to go. A spray of water rained down on him. It came from behind. He shouted with surprise and looked back.

The elephant's trunk was pointed straight at Annie.

"Cool!" she cried. "He's giving me a shower!"

The elephant sprayed her again...then again. The mud slowly rolled off her face, her braids, her T-shirt, her shorts, her legs, and her sneakers.

"I guess the elephant doesn't like dirty kids!" said Annie, laughing. Her eyes were squeezed shut.

Finally, she was clean and soaking wet.

"Now it's your turn," she said to Jack.

Jack stepped forward and shut his eyes tight. A blast of water hit him. It *did* feel like a shower—a strong shower.

When Jack was clean, the elephant let out a grunt. Then he started to splash himself with water.

"Thanks!" said Annie.

"Yeah, thanks!" said Jack.

"I'm spick-and-span now," said Annie.

"When the sun dries me off, I'll be like new."

"Good," said Jack. "Now we can get serious."

He picked up his heavy pack. "We have to figure out the answer to the riddle. So we can leave this place...before we run into real trouble."

He looked around nervously. *Where are the lions?* he wondered.

A small bird flitted near his head.

"Hi," Annie said to the bird.

Jack turned back to her. "According to the riddle, we're looking for something gold and sweet."

"What do you want?" Annie asked the bird.

The bird twittered and flew around Jack and Annie. Its feathers were dull gray. But it had a bright, happy manner.

"Annie, listen to *me*, not the bird," said Jack.

The bird kept fluttering around them.

"She's trying to tell us something," said Annie.

Jack let out a long sigh. "You are driving me crazy today," he said.

"But I feel like she needs our help," said Annie. "Maybe her babies fell out of the nest."

"Annie, you can't save every animal in Africa," said Jack.

"This bird is important," said Annie. "Trust me."

The bird darted toward the trees. It landed on a branch and cocked its head at them.

"She says *follow*," said Annie.

The bird headed into the forest. Annie started after it.

"*Don't* go in there!" said Jack. "You might run into—"

There was no need to finish. The bird and Annie had disappeared into the trees.

"—a snake or a lion," Jack said to himself.

"Come on!" Annie called.

Jack moaned. He pulled on his pack and ran. The peanut butter jar thumped against his back.

7

Hi, There

The forest was cooler than the sunny plains. It was filled with shadows and bird calls.

"Where are you?" Jack shouted.

"Here!" said Annie.

He found her in a thick glade.

Bright rays streamed between the trees. Green leaves and vines swayed in the dappled light.

The little gray bird sat in a tree, twittering at them.

"Yuck, what's that?" said Annie. She pointed at a round brown thing hanging from a low branch. Bees buzzed around it.

"If that's her nest, it's a pretty weird nest," said Annie.

"That's not a nest," said Jack. "It's a beehive. Don't you see the bees?"

"Yikes," said Annie. She stepped back from the tree.

But the little bird darted at the beehive and pecked at it.

"What's she doing?" said Annie.

The bird kept pecking at the hive.

"I don't know. Maybe she's as nuts as you," said Jack.

"Look her up in the book," said Annie. "See if it says she's nuts."

"Are you kidding?" said Jack. "That nutty

bird isn't going to be in this book."

"Just look."

Jack opened his Africa book. He kept turning the pages. Just as he thought—there was no gray bird in the book.

"Forget it," he said.

"Keep looking," said Annie.

Jack turned one more page. And there it was: a little gray bird, a beehive, and a tall, painted warrior with a spear.

"I don't believe this," said Jack.

Then he read aloud:

>**This bird is called a honey guide. It's both a friend and a helper to the Masai (muh-SI) people, an African tribe known for their fierce fighting skills and bravery.**

"Hi, honey guide," Annie called to the bird. "I *knew* you were important."

Jack kept reading:

> The honey guide leads a Masai
> tribesperson to a beehive. The bird
> waits for him or her to scatter the bees
> and take the honey. Then the bird
> feasts on the honeycomb.

"That's cool," said Jack. "They work together, like the zebras and wildebeests and gazelles."

"Yeah," said Annie. "And she wants *us* to be her helpers. We have to scatter the bees and leave her the honeycomb."

"How do we do that?" said Jack. He looked back at the book. It didn't say how.

"Well, maybe we could wave those weeds

at them," said Annie. She pointed to some bright green plants that looked like giant fans.

Jack put his book and backpack down. He and Annie pulled up the weeds. They waved them near the tree, and the bees scattered.

Next, Jack grabbed the tree branch and jiggled it. The hive fell to the ground and broke open.

Annie stooped and stuck her finger into the golden honeycomb.

"Yummy," she said when she tasted the honey. "Try it."

Jack stuck his finger in the honeycomb,

too. He licked off the golden honey. It was the sweetest honey he had ever tasted.

"Now the honey guide can get to her honeycomb," said Annie.

"Yeah, but she'd better hurry. Before the bees come back," said Jack.

"It's weird," said Annie. "Honey's so sweet and good. But to get it, you have to go past a lot of dangerous bees."

"Oh, man," whispered Jack. *That's it.*

"That's what?" asked Annie.

Jack said Morgan's riddle:

> I'm the color of gold
> and as sweet as can be.
> But beware of the danger
> that's all around me.
> What am I?

"I get it," Annie whispered. "Honey..."

"Honey," said Jack, nodding and smiling. "That's it. We've answered Morgan's riddle. Let's go home."

He stood up to leave. He gasped.

Standing in the shadows was a tall man with a spear and a curved sword hanging from his belt. His face was painted in fierce, bright colors.

Jack knew at once what he was.

A Masai warrior.

"Hi, there," Annie said in a small voice.

8

Yum

The warrior stared back at Jack and Annie.

"We were helping one of your honey guides," said Annie.

The warrior was as still as a statue.

"We didn't mean to steal anything," Jack said. "In fact, it's all yours. We've had enough."

"Lots of good honey still there," Annie said, smiling.

The warrior narrowed his eyes.

Is he angry? Jack wondered.

"I'm sorry we were trespassing," said Jack. "We come in peace. In fact, we bring gifts." He picked up his backpack and held it out to the warrior.

The warrior still didn't move.

"This?" Jack held up his book.

Nothing.

"Uh—" Jack reached into his pack. He pulled out the big jar of peanut butter.

"Peanut butter!" He pulled out the loaf of bread. "Bread! Hey. Hey! How about a peanut butter and honey sandwich?"

"Yum!" Annie said, watching the warrior.

The warrior stared at the food.

"We'll show you," said Jack.

As Jack unwrapped the bread, his hands shook.

Annie opened the jar.

"We don't have anything to spread it with," she said.

"Use your fingers," said Jack.

"Excuse me," Annie said to the warrior. "I have to use my fingers. But they're pretty clean. An elephant just—"

"Just do it, Annie!" said Jack.

"Okay, okay."

She spread the peanut butter onto a slice of bread with her fingers. At the same time, Jack spread the honey from the beehive on another slice.

Jack and Annie put their pieces of bread together.

"Ta-da!" said Annie, handing the sandwich to the warrior.

The warrior took the sandwich, but he

didn't eat it. He just looked at it.

"Let's make sandwiches for us, too," Jack said. "So he doesn't have to eat alone."

They quickly made two more sandwiches.

"See, like this," said Annie. She bit into her sandwich. "Mmm...yum."

Jack took a bite, too. "Mmm..." he said. It *was* really good.

Finally, the warrior bit into his sandwich. He chewed slowly.

"This is called a picnic," said Annie.

They ate their sandwiches in silence.

When they finished, Jack screwed the lid back on the peanut butter jar.

"Not bad, huh?" he said.

The warrior smiled. He had a kind, dignified smile.

Jack and Annie smiled back at him.

Then the warrior turned gracefully and vanished into the trees.

"Oh, man," said Jack. Part of him wanted to follow the silent warrior through the shadowy forest.

"Ready?" Annie asked softly.

Jack nodded.

Annie started to go.

"Wait," said Jack. He put away the peanut butter and bread. "We're going back to the tree house, right? We're not going to do anything silly, like rescue anything or chase birds. Right?"

"Those things aren't silly," said Annie. "Don't forget that the bird gave us the answer to the riddle."

"Oh. Right," said Jack.

He looked at the little honey guide. She

was on the ground, pecking at the honey-comb.

"Thanks," Jack said to the bird.

"Have a good feast," said Annie.

Jack put on his pack. Then he and Annie started out of the forest.

When they passed the pond, they saw the elephant still splashing in the water. He lifted his trunk. He seemed to be waving at them.

"See ya!" Annie shouted, waving back.

They rounded the bend in the river, then started through the tall grass.

As they walked back toward the tree house, they saw the wildebeests in the distance. There were still some crossing the river.

They saw a family of zebras grazing together.

They saw lone giraffes walking from tree to tree, eating the leaves.

And they saw a bunch of lions sleeping in the shade of a tree—*the same tree that the tree house was in.*

"Whoops," said Annie.

Jack's heart gave a jump.

"So *there* they are," he said.

9

Tiptoe

Jack and Annie crouched in the tall grass. There was a big lion, three lionesses, and a bunch of cubs.

"I think they're sleeping," whispered Annie.

"Yeah," said Jack. "But for how long?"

He pulled the Africa book from his pack and opened it. He found a picture of lions sleeping under a tree.

He read in a whispery voice:

**After a pride of lions has eaten, they
rest for a few hours. The other—**

"What did they have for lunch?" Annie
broke in.

"Don't ask," said Jack. He kept reading:

**Sensing that the lions are not hunting
at the moment, the other animals graze
nearby.**

"If they can graze, then we're safe," said
Annie. She started to stand.

"Wait!" Jack pulled her down. "Not so
fast."

He peered around. The words in the book
seemed true: the zebras and giraffes didn't
seem to be bothered by the lions at all.

"They might be safe. But I'm not sure
about us," said Jack. "We need a plan."

"What if we wait till they leave?" said Annie.

"That could take hours," said Jack. "Plus they might be hungry again by then."

"Oh, right," said Annie.

"So here's the plan—we tiptoe," said Jack.

"Tiptoe?"

"Yeah?"

"That's your whole plan?" said Annie.

"Yeah, tiptoe to the rope ladder," said Jack. "Very quietly."

"Good plan," Annie teased.

"Just do it," said Jack. He stood up slowly. Annie stood with him.

They began tiptoeing through the grass very slowly.

The lion flicked his tail.

Jack and Annie froze.

When his tail was still again, they moved again.

Suddenly, high-pitched laughter split the air.

Jack and Annie stopped.

The hyenas were back! They were standing off to the side, watching Jack and Annie.

Jack and Annie made silent monster faces

and shook their fists. But the hyenas only laughed some more.

The big lion stirred lazily. He opened his golden eyes.

Jack felt the hair rise on the back of his neck. But he didn't move an inch.

The lion lifted his head and yawned. His giant teeth gleamed in the sunlight. The lion turned his head as he looked around sleepily.

Jack held his breath as the lion's gaze rested on him. The lion sat straight up. His piercing yellow eyes met Jack's.

Jack's heart raced. His mind raced. He remembered something he'd read—*lions avoid giraffes*.

Jack looked around. There was a giraffe walking toward the tree that the magic tree house was in.

Suddenly, he had a *new* plan.

"Get under that giraffe," he whispered.

"Now *you're* the one who's nuts," Annie whispered back.

But Jack grabbed her hand. He pulled her over to the giraffe and underneath it.

The giraffe's legs were so long, Jack and Annie could stand up under it. Jack's head barely brushed the giraffe's golden belly.

The tall creature froze for a few seconds. Then she moved slowly toward the tree.

Jack and Annie walked in the same rhythm as the giraffe.

They got closer and closer to the tree house—and closer and closer to the pride of lions.

The big lion had stood up. He watched them moving under the giraffe.

When the rope ladder was just a few feet away, Jack and Annie dashed out from under the giraffe to the rope ladder.

Annie scrambled up first.

Jack followed right behind her.

As they climbed, the lion growled and leaped at the ladder.

The hyenas laughed.

Jack climbed faster than he'd ever climbed. He leaped after Annie into the tree house.

Annie had already unrolled the scroll. The riddle was gone. In its place was one shimmering word:

HONEY

Jack grabbed the Pennsylvania book. He opened it and found the picture of the Frog Creek woods.

"Iwishwecouldgothere!" he said.

Just then, the giraffe stuck her head through the window.

"Bye, *honey!*" said Annie, and she kissed the giraffe on the nose.

The wind started to blow.

The tree house started to spin.

It spun faster and faster.

Then everything was still.

Absolutely still.

10

After Lunch

Jack opened his eyes. His heart was still racing. Hyena laughter still rang in his ears.

"We made it," said Annie.

"Yes," said Jack. "But it was very close."

Jack took another moment to calm down. Then he pulled the Africa book out of his pack and put it with the other books.

Annie put the scroll with the other two scrolls.

"The giraffe was the *true* honey on that

trip," she said, "sweet and golden, with danger all around it."

"Yep," Jack said. "And now we have just one riddle to go."

"Yep," said Annie. "Ready?"

"Ready."

She started down the ladder. Jack followed. When they hit the ground, they walked through the sunlit woods.

"It's time for lunch," said Jack.

"I'm full from our picnic," said Annie.

"Same here," said Jack.

"What do we tell Mom?" said Annie.

"We say we ate our sandwiches coming back from the store," said Jack.

"What if she asks *why?*" said Annie.

"Oh...just say we had a picnic with a Masai warrior in Africa," said Jack.

Annie laughed. "Right," she said, "because we didn't want him to be mad at us for taking his honey."

"Right," said Jack, "the honey from a bee-hive that a honey guide led us to."

"Right," said Annie, "and that happened *after* an elephant gave me a shower. And we scared off two hyenas."

"Right," said Jack, "and after you fell into a mudhole because you were helping a million wildebeests migrate across a river."

"Right," said Annie. "And *all* that was before a giraffe saved us from a lion."

"Right," said Jack.

Jack and Annie left the Frog Creek woods and started up their sunny street.

They were silent for a moment.

Then Jack pushed his glasses into place.

"We better just say we ate our sandwiches on the way home from the store," he said.

"Right," said Annie.

"And if Mom asks why—" started Jack.

"We'll just say it's a really long story," said Annie.

"Right," said Jack, "with, like—ten chapters."

Annie laughed. "Good plan," she said.

"*Very* good plan," said Jack.

They crossed their yard. They went up their steps and through their front door.

"We're back!" Annie shouted.

"Great!" called their mom. "Ready for lunch?"

Read about how Jack and Annie find the
answer to the final riddle in the snow and ice
of Alaska in

MAGIC TREE HOUSE   #12

POLAR BEARS
PAST BEDTIME

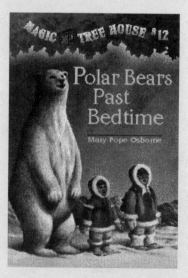